READ ME A STORY

Bedtime tales

𝑝

Ursula's Umbrella

Ursula was a little girl who longed for adventure. She loved reading stories about far-away places and explorers, and even children like herself who had amazing adventures. "Why doesn't anything interesting ever happen to me?" she sighed. "How I wish I could fly to the moon or dive to the deepest part of the ocean. What fun it would be!"

One windy day, Ursula went out for a walk. She took her umbrella with her because it looked as though it might be going to rain. Ursula's umbrella was red with a shiny black handle. It was also very large indeed. People used to laugh as Ursula walked along the street with her umbrella up. It looked so big and Ursula was so small that it seemed as though the umbrella was walking along all by itself!

As Ursula walked up the street she felt a few raindrops on her nose. "Better put up my umbrella," she thought. She unfurled her umbrella and lifted it up above her head. As she did so, a great gust of wind came and swept her right off the pavement. It carried her past the upstairs windows of the houses, past the roofs and the chimney pots and up, up, into the sky. Ursula clung tightly to the umbrella handle. She was surprised to find she didn't feel the least bit frightened. No, not a bit. She felt very excited. She looked down and saw streets and factories whizzing past far below. Then she saw fields and something that looked like a silver thread snaking through the countryside. "A river!" thought Ursula.

Now she could see the coastline, and soon the umbrella was carrying her out over the ocean. At first when she looked down the sea was grey, but gradually it turned to the deepest blue with frothy white waves. "How I'd love a swim," thought Ursula. At that moment she felt the umbrella starting to descend. Looking down she could see that they were heading for an island in the middle of the ocean. Soon she was floating past the tops of palm trees and, as she touched the ground, she felt sand under her feet.

"I'm going for a swim!" said Ursula to herself. She folded up her umbrella and set off to the beach. The water felt deliciously warm as Ursula paddled about. She looked down and saw that the water was amazingly clear. She could see brightly coloured fish darting in and out of the coral. "Wow!" exclaimed Ursula out loud and then "Wow!" again, though this time much louder as she looked up and saw a black fin skimming through the water towards her. "Shark!" she shrieked, but no-one heard.

Then all of a sudden a gust of wind made her umbrella unfurl itself and float towards her in the water, like a boat. Ursula made a dash for the umbrella, hurled herself into it and floated away across the sea. "That was quite an adventure!" she thought.

After a while, Ursula looked out over the rim of the umbrella and saw that it was heading for the shore again. This time, when Ursula stepped out of the umbrella, she found that she was at the edge of a jungle. Folding up the umbrella, she set off into the forest. She followed an overgrown path through the trees. "I wonder where this leads?" thought Ursula. She wiped her brow and swatted the insects that flew in front of her face. Deeper and deeper into the jungle she went.

Suddenly she heard the sound of rushing water and found herself standing on the banks of a river. All at once she heard another sound. It was the crashing noise of some enormous beast approaching through the trees.

5

Where could she run to? Suddenly she felt the umbrella being blown from her hand. To her amazement it fell to the ground, stretching right across the river like a bridge. Ursula walked over to the other side, not daring to look down at the torrent below. When she was safely on the far bank she looked back to see a large puma, with glittering green eyes, glaring at her from the opposite bank. "That was a lucky escape!" thought Ursula.

Ursula could see a mountain through the trees and decided to head towards it. "I'll be able to get a good view from the top and maybe find my way home," she thought. She struggled on through the forest and eventually found herself at the foot of the mountain. There seemed to be no way up the sheer rock face.

Ursula was on the point of despair when suddenly another great gust of wind blew up. It carried Ursula, clinging to her opened umbrella, all the way up to the top of the mountain.

URSULA'S UMBRELLA

At the top of the mountain, the umbrella let her gently down again and her feet landed in deep snow. By now it was blowing a blizzard and she could not see anything except white snowflakes in all directions. "There's only one thing to do," thought Ursula. She put the umbrella on the snow, sat on it and whizzed all the way down the other side of the mountain.

When she reached the bottom, to her surprise, the umbrella sledge didn't stop but carried on through the snowstorm until eventually, after a very long time, it came to a halt right outside her own front door. "Well, that was quite an adventure," said Ursula, shaking the snow off the umbrella, before folding it up.

She stepped inside the front door. "Wherever have you been?" said her mother. "You look as though you've been to the ends of the Earth and back."

"Well I have," Ursula was about to say. But then she thought that no-one would believe her and it was nicer to keep her adventures to herself. And that is what she did.

The Mirror of Dreams

The house on the corner of Nightingale Avenue was tall and very handsome, and was by far the largest in the neighbourhood. From the street you could see four floors of beautifully decorated rooms, and if you peeped over the railings you could see the basement below. If you were lucky enough to be asked into the house, and passed through the beautiful hallways into the playroom, you might meet the owner's daughter, Cordelia. Sometimes Cordelia would be sitting in her silk pyjamas playing on her grand piano, and sometimes she would be dressed in the finest velvet gowns playing with her lovely dolls.

If you went down the stairs and into the basement, you might come across Polly. Polly's mother was a chambermaid in the house, and worked hard all day long to make the house sparkling clean. Sometimes Polly helped her to polish the ornaments and dust the furniture, but more often Polly sat on her own in her small bedroom drawing pictures with some crayons on a drawing pad she had been given for her birthday. When Polly was helping to polish the furniture she would look longingly at all of

Cordelia's fine clothes and toys, and when she sat alone in her room she would draw pictures of all the beautiful things she would like to own if only she could afford them.

One day, a large parcel was delivered to the house and taken upstairs to Cordelia's bedroom. A little while later, Cordelia's maid carried a pretty, ornate mirror down from her room and put it with the rubbish waiting for collection outside the house. Polly asked the maid why the mirror was to be thrown away, and the maid explained that Cordelia had been given a new mirror in which to brush her long, silky locks, and that she didn't need it any more. The maid then asked if Polly would like the old mirror, and of course Polly accepted with pleasure – it was the most beautiful thing she had ever owned.

Polly carried the mirror back to her room and polished it lovingly. As she polished the glass a strange thing started to happen. The glass went misty, and then cleared as her own reflection stared back at her once more. But the reflection that stared back was not dressed in rags and worn old clothes as Polly was, but in a rich gown of the most beautiful cream satin, with pink bows and apricot lace.

Polly was entranced. She looked almost as beautiful as Cordelia! Her hair gleamed and her fingers were white and magnificent. As she looked further into the mirror, she saw herself dancing at a ball, and then sitting down to eat the finest food she had ever seen – hams and roasted meats, and cakes of strawberries and cream!

And then the mirror spoke to her. "I am the Mirror of Dreams," the cool, clear voice said. "Whatever your heart desires most will be reflected in my shiny surface."

Polly was astounded, but so happy. She didn't care that it was only a day dream, for when she saw her reflection in the beautiful clothes, she felt as if she were truly there dancing and eating the fine foods – she could almost taste the fruit and cream in her mouth!

From that day on, Polly sat in her room every day, and dreamed and dreamed and dreamed. She had never felt so happy before, and could not wait to wake up each morning to visit her imaginary world. She certainly didn't understand how Cordelia could have thrown away such a magical wonder, and thought that she could not have known of its enchanting secret. She supposed also that Cordelia could have had no use for such a mirror, for whatever Cordelia wanted in real life she received, and would have no need to dream. But Polly was to find out that this was very far from true!

Weeks passed, and every day Polly sat and dreamed of ermine cloaks, of diamonds and pearls, of parties and picnics and carnivals. Eventually, she had dreamed every dream she had ever wanted. And Polly began to realise that it no longer made her as happy as it once had, and she began to grow weary of her Mirror of Dreams. She sat in front of the mirror less and less, and eventually when she did visit the mirror she could not think of a single thing that would make her happy. Even the dreams she had in which her mother wore fine silk clothes and didn't have to scrub and clean for their living could no longer make her happy.

She preferred her real mother, who came to kiss her good night and read her stories no matter how tired and overworked she was. Eventually she stopped looking in the mirror altogether, and finally decided to throw the mirror away – it had only made her more unhappy.

As the long winter turned into spring she acted upon her decision, and took down the mirror to throw away with the rubbish. But as she looked into the glass, it misted over in its familiar way and she saw herself in the mirror as she looked in real life, but in it she was playing with other children like herself, and reading stories with them and sharing toys. She felt gloriously happy, and knew in that instant that all she wanted was a very good friend. She realised in that moment, too, that perhaps Cordelia really had known the mirror's secret, but that she also had become more unhappy as the dreams faded and reality forced itself upon her. She wondered aloud what it was that Cordelia had dreamed of, and for the second and last time the mirror spoke in its cool, clear voice.

"The Mirror of Dreams showed Cordelia her heart's desire, and her heart desires a true friend and companion – someone who is not jealous of her wealth, but a friend who will share her hopes and dreams, and with whom she can have parties, games and picnics."

Polly put the mirror down and thought with amazement that she could be that friend, if Cordelia would be friends with someone poor but honest and true. Polly left the mirror with the household rubbish and was about to make the descent back to the basement, when she saw Cordelia standing in the garden at the back of the house. Cordelia had seen her discard the mirror, and shyly walked up to Polly. Polly overcame her shyness also and went to meet Cordelia, and then she told her they shared the same dream.

Cordelia and Polly became the best of friends from that day on. They shared everything they had, no matter how much or little. They talked and laughed together all day long, and they played long into the evening. They didn't have to dream any more, for they had both got their true heart's desire.

The Giant Who Shrank

Once upon a time in a far-off land, there lived a huge giant.
He made his home in a big cave high up in the mountains.
His bed, table and chairs were made from great tree trunks.
And when he wanted a drink, he simply filled an old bath tub
with water and drank it down in one enormous gulp.
When he snored – which he did almost every night –
it sounded like a huge thunderstorm,
and the noise echoed all
around the mountains.

At the bottom of the mountains there was a village, but all the folk in the village were very different from the giant, for they were not big at all. They were just like you and me. They were afraid of the giant, of course, and whenever he came striding down the mountains to hunt, they all ran away into the woods or locked themselves inside their houses. Sometimes, the clumsy giant would tramp around the village squashing houses with his great feet as he went, and that only made the village folk even more frightened of him!

Although the giant was so big and strong, he was not a bad giant, but he was very, very lonely because everyone ran away whenever he appeared. Sometimes, while he was sitting alone in his cave, he could hear the villagers having feasts and parties and he longed to join them and be just like them.

One day, when the giant was tramping around the village as usual, something glinting in the sun caught his eye. At the top of a big tree (which of course was not very big as far as the giant was concerned) lay a gold box.

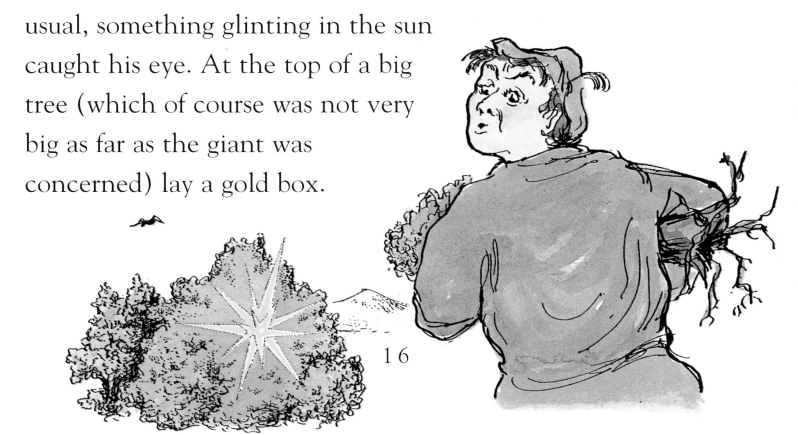

16

The giant bent down and picked up the box. To his surprise he heard a small voice inside say, "Help! Help! Let me out!"

The giant opened the box and out jumped an elf. "Thank you, thank you, large sir," he said. "I am a magic elf, but one of my spells went wrong and I got locked inside this box. No-one in the village could hear me calling for help high up in this tree."

To show his thanks, the elf said he would grant the giant one wish.

"I wish I could be the same as all the other villagers," boomed the giant.

"What a difficult wish," said the elf. "You are so big! But I will do my best." The elf closed his eyes and chanted a magic spell. But nothing seemed to happen – the giant was still as big as ever.

17

The giant was very sad to discover that he had not shrunk, but he wished the elf well, thanked him for trying and went on his way. As the giant was walking back to his cave in the mountains, he noticed something strange. All the puddles of water that he had passed on the way down to the village had got bigger. They were as big as lakes now! The giant looked up to see if it had been raining, but the sky was clear and blue.

Then another strange thing happened. The big stone steps he had cut in the mountain side leading up to his cave had also got bigger! He could hardly clamber up them.

Eventually, puffing and panting, the giant reached the door to his cave. But he could not reach the door knob. It now towered above him, far from his reach.

"What is happening?" thought the giant. "The elf's spell must have gone wrong. Not only am I still a giant, but everything around me has now got even bigger."

Suddenly the truth came to him. Of course! Everything had not become bigger – he had become smaller! The spell had worked after all. Now he was just the same as the other folk in the village.

He made his way to the village, wondering if everyone would still run away as before. But he need not have worried. All the village folk welcomed him into the village, and he lived there happily among them for the rest of his days.

19

Morag the Witch

Morag was just an ordinary witch – until the day she enrolled for a course of advanced spell casting at the Wizard, Witch and Warlock Institute of Magic. For that was where she met Professor Fizzlestick. Now Professor Fizzlestick was a very wise old man indeed. Morag, on the other hand, was a very vain young witch who didn't know as much as she thought she did. She could turn people into frogs if they really deserved it, and do other simple spells like that, but she still had a lot to learn. The problem was, Morag thought she was the most perfect little witch in the whole wide world.

Morag's adventure started on her very first day at school. At the beginning of the day, after all the young witches and wizards had made friends and met the teachers, they were called in one by one to talk to Professor Fizzlestick.

"Now, young Morag Bendlebaum, I taught both your mother and your father," said the professor in a very serious voice, "and a very fine witch and wizard they turned out to be, too. So, what kind of witch do you think you are going to be?"

Without giving this any thought at all, Morag blurted out, "I'm better than my parents, and I'm probably better than you!"

This answer surprised even Morag, for although she thought this was true, she didn't actually mean to say it.

"Don't be surprised by your answers," said Professor Fizzlestick, "there is a truth spell in this room, and whatever you truly believe you must say. And I have to say that you appear to have an enormously high opinion of yourself. Why don't you tell me what makes you so very good?"

"I'm clever," said Morag, "and I'm good, and I'm always right."

"But what about your dark side?" said Professor Fizzlestick.

"I'm sorry to disappoint you," replied Morag quite seriously, "but I'm afraid I simply don't have a dark side."

21

"Well in that case I would like you to meet someone very close to you," said Professor Fizzlestick with a smile on his lips.

Morag looked over to where Professor Fizzlestick pointed, and was startled to see on the sofa next to her... herself!

As Morag stared open-mouthed with astonishment, the professor explained that if, as she believed, she was without a dark side, then there was absolutely nothing to worry about. "If, however," he continued, "you have deceived yourself, then I'm afraid you are in for a few surprises."

With that the professor dismissed them both from the room and told them to get to know each other. As Morag and her dark side stood outside the professor's room, Morag's dark side jumped and whooped for joy. "At last," she cried, "I'm free. I don't have to sit and listen to you telling me what's right all day; I don't have to keep persuading you to choose the biggest slice of cake before your brother – in fact, I don't, I repeat **don't,** have to do anything that you tell me at all."

So saying she broke into a run and rushed down the corridor, knocking over chairs and bumping into other little witches and wizards along the way. Morag was horrified. She would have to follow her dark side and stop her from causing trouble. Morag chased after her dark side and finally caught up with her at the chocolate machine. "Don't eat all that chocolate," cried Morag. "You know it's bad for your teeth and will ruin your appetite for lunch!"

"Tsk!" scoffed her dark side. "You might not want any chocolate but I certainly do!" And with that she ran off once more, dropping chocolate on to the freshly polished floor as well as pushing a big piece into her mouth.

Just then, the bell sounded for lunch. Although Morag felt she ought to find her dark side, she also knew that the bell was a command to go to the dining hall, and she mustn't disobey it. Morag sat down to lunch next to her friend, Topaz. She was just about to tell her what had happened, when she saw that Topaz was not eating her vegetables! Morag scolded Topaz for this, and gave her a lecture on eating healthily.

Topaz stared at Morag in amazement, then peered closely at her. "What's happened to you?" she asked.

Morag explained what had happened in Professor Fizzlestick's office, and then declared, "And you know, it's the best thing that has ever happened to me. I thought I was good before, but now I'm even better. I never want my dark side back again, but we must find her and lock her up so that she can do no harm."

Topaz agreed that they must find her dark side, but secretly hoped that she and Morag would be re-united. Morag wasn't Morag without her dark side.

After lunch, Morag went for her first lesson of the afternoon. When she walked into the classroom she discovered her dark side already there, busy preparing spells! Morag's dark side had already prepared a 'turning a nose into an elephant's trunk' spell and a 'turning skin into dragons' scales' spell and was just finishing off a 'turning your teacher into stone' spell!

Morag suddenly heard a trumpeting noise from the back of the classroom. She turned to find that the wizard twins, Denzil and Dorian Dillydally, had both sprouted huge grey trunks down to the ground where their noses had been. Morag rushed over to her dark side to make her change them back, but before she could reach her she tripped over a creature crouching down on the floor. It looked just like a dragon and it was wearing a purple and white spotted dress last seen on Betina Bumblebag. Morag's dark side was casting spells all over the place. "Oh, why doesn't the teacher stop her!" cried Morag to Topaz.

I'm sure you've guessed by now. Nice Miss Chuckle was entirely turned to stone from head to foot!

Just then Professor Fizzlestick walked into the classroom. Morag pointed to her dark side, still making spells at the front of the classroom.

24

"Lock her up immediately," Morag begged the professor.

"I'm afraid that you are the only one who can do that," said the wise old man. "The two of you are inseparable and you need each other. Without your dark side you would be unbearable and without you she is dreadful. Have I your permission to lock her back inside you?"

Even though Morag didn't want any part of her dark side back, she agreed reluctantly. Her dark side instantly disappeared, and Morag felt... wonderful! Oh, it was so good to be back to normal, to be basically good, but occasionally mischievous.

"Thank you," said Morag to the professor. "I think I've learned something very valuable today."

"There is good and bad in everyone," replied the professor, "even the most perfect of witches."

Morag blushed when she remembered what she had said earlier that morning, but she was so relieved to find she was normal that she really didn't mind. Morag and Topaz went back to the classroom to undo all the bad things Morag's dark side had done, but on the way they both felt a huge urge for a snack, so they stopped at the chocolate machine first!

No Hunting!

Mr Rabbit opened his eyes and gave a big yawn. He thought it seemed like the perfect day for going outside and nibbling some of the farmer's lettuces. And after that he thought he would go and see how well the farmer's carrots were growing, and maybe have a little nibble of those as well. He popped his head out of his burrow and looked this way and that, in case he saw any danger. Then he pricked up his ears and turned this way and that, in case he heard any danger. Finally, he sniffed the air this way and that, in case he smelled any danger. It seemed safe, so he hopped out of his burrow.

No sooner had he gone a couple of steps when "ZING" – a bullet whizzed past his head. Mr Rabbit jumped back into his burrow as fast as he could go, shaking with fright.

"Goodness, it's the rabbit hunting season," he gasped. He gathered his family of young rabbits around him and spoke to them. "Now children, listen very carefully," he said. "The rabbit hunting season has begun, so you must all stay safely inside the burrow until it's over. I will go out at night and forage for food for us all."

His children looked at him in dismay. "But it's lovely and sunny outside," they cried all together. "We'll be very careful."

But Mr Rabbit was having none of it. He insisted that they all stay under ground until the rabbit season was over.

For a few days, the young rabbits amused themselves as best they could by playing chase and hide and seek. But they were becoming very bored. Finally, they decided that they were going to do something to stop the rabbit hunting themselves.

First Tom, the eldest of Mr Rabbit's children, decided he would try and stop the hunters. So when it was dark, he crept out of the burrow and made his way towards the hunters' hut.

Although it was night and he was sure the hunters would be asleep, he was still very scared. Soon he came to the hut. It was standing in a clearing in the woods. It was dark inside the hut and he hoped the hunters were asleep. "If I can dig some big holes," he thought, "maybe they will fall into them in the morning and won't be able to get out until the hunting season is over."

So he dug and he dug like he had never dug before. Soon there were holes everywhere, right outside the door to the hunters' hut. Feeling very pleased with himself, but also very tired, Tom made his way back to the burrow just before it was light.

When the hunters awoke, they went straight out without falling down a single hole! Poor Tom, he had dug lots of holes alright, but the hunters' hut had two doors, and the hunters had simply gone out of the other one!

Then Jenny, the second oldest of Mr Rabbit's children, decided that she would try and stop the hunters. So when it was dark, she crept out of the burrow and made her way towards the hunters' hut. When she got there, she noticed that the window was open and so she decided to go inside. She, too, was very scared, but she thought about having to spend all those days in the burrow until the hunting season was over and that gave her the courage to carry on.

Inside the hut, she could see the hunters sleeping in their beds. She looked around, wondering what she could do to stop them hunting. Then suddenly she saw the hunters' clothes lying on a chair. Quick as a flash, she hopped up to them and started nibbling at them. In no time at all, the clothes were in shreds. "That'll stop them," thought Jenny. "They can't hunt without their clothes on!" Satisfied with her night's work, Jenny made her way back to the burrow just as dawn was breaking.

When the hunters awoke, they got straight up and went out hunting! Poor Jenny, she had chewed some clothes alright, but she had only chewed some spare clothes! The hunters had gone to bed wearing their other clothes in order to be out quickly in the morning.

Finally, Penelope, the youngest of Mr Rabbit's children, said she would try and stop the hunters.

"Don't be silly," said Tom to his sister. "You are far too young to be going out at night."

"And anyway," said Jenny, "what could you possibly think of doing to stop the hunters?"

"I'll think of something," said Penelope, who was really quite a clever little rabbit.

So that night, she crept out of the burrow and made her way to the hunters' hut. The window was open, just as before, and so Penelope hopped inside. She looked on the floor, she looked in the cupboards, and she looked under the beds, but she couldn't think of anything to stop the hunters.

Then she looked up and suddenly had an idea. For there on the table was a calendar, showing that very day's date. Penelope hopped on to the table and started to turn the pages. Finally she came to a page on the calendar that read: "RABBIT HUNTING SEASON ENDS TODAY". Satisfied with her work, Penelope hopped out of the hunters' hut and back home to her burrow.

In the morning, the hunters woke up, rubbed their eyes and got out of their beds. One of them glanced at the calendar. "Oh no!" he suddenly exclaimed. "Look at the date! The rabbit hunting season is over."

With that, the hunters (who were too silly to realise that someone else must have turned over the pages of the calendar) packed their belongings and went home. All was peace and quiet once more and the rabbits could hop about in the open air in safety.

Cinderella

Once upon a time there was a beautiful young girl who lived with her widowed father. He had brought her up to be kind and gentle. All went well until the day the girl's father married again. His second wife was very proud of her house. Everything always had to be spotlessly clean. Worse than that, she had two spiteful daughters. All three had terrible tempers, and they hated the beautiful young girl with a vengeance. All day long from dawn to dusk she was made to scrub and clean, mend clothes and serve at the table. At night, while the household slept, there was coal to fetch, fires to be laid and the table to be set for breakfast the following day.

The stepmother gave her own two daughters the finest rooms in the house. To her stepdaughter, she gave the coldest attic room, with the hardest bed and a quilt cover that was so thin it barely kept out the winter chill. To keep warm, the poor girl had to sit in the chimney nook of the kitchen with her feet near the cinders. Because of this, her stepsisters nicknamed her Cinderella.

One day a footman called at the house to deliver an invitation. Cinderella carried it into the dining room where her stepsisters were having breakfast. "What have you there?" shrieked one of them, snatching the envelope from her hand. She tore it open with her long, polished nails. "Ooh!" she cried. "It's an invitation from the prince to attend a ball tomorrow night!"

The other sister jumped up and down with delight. "We're going to a ball!" she yelled.

"Am I invited, too?" asked Cinderella shyly.

"You?" cried the elder sister.

"You – invited to the palace ball?" cried the other sister, and they both burst into fits of laughter. The elder sister, who was very plump, laughed so much that she became quite breathless and had to ask Cinderella to loosen her corset.

The sisters spent the next day preparing for the ball. Cinderella was kept very busy, pressing and starching the girls' ballgowns, curling their hair and fixing bows and ribbons. They told her to lace their corsets extra tight to make them look slimmer. She was made to run hither and thither all day. "Fetch my pearl necklace!" called one.

"Polish my party shoes!" demanded the other. At last both sisters were ready to go, and set off by carriage to the ball. "Don't wait up!" they shouted out of the window to Cinderella, as the coach sped away.

Cinderella went back into the kitchen. Now the house seemed calm and quiet at last. She picked up a broom and danced slowly round the room, imagining that she was at the ball. "How wonderful it would be to go to the ball," she sighed wistfully, and sat down by the fire where it was warm and started to cry.

"Don't cry, my child," said a gentle voice.

Cinderella looked up to see a beautiful stranger standing before her. "Who are you?" said Cinderella.

"I am your fairy godmother," came the reply. "Now, dry your tears. Would you like to go to the ball?" said the fairy.

"Oh, yes please," cried Cinderella, leaping up.

"Then you shall go," said the fairy. "But first, run into the garden, and fetch me a nice fat pumpkin." Cinderella did as she was told. When she returned, the fairy godmother tapped the pumpkin with her magic wand and instantly it was transformed into a sparkling glass coach.

"Now we need some horses," said the fairy. At that moment there was a scuttling noise in the corner of the kitchen and four white mice popped out of a hole. In an instant the fairy godmother tapped them with her wand and they became four handsome white horses. "Now what about a footman," she said. Before Cinderella could speak she tapped Cinderella's black cat and there before her very eyes stood a footman. "Now there's just one more thing we need before you go," said the fairy, "and that's a coachman."

Cinderella looked about the kitchen and scratched her head.

Then she ran into the garden and came back with a live frog. "Will he do?" she asked her fairy godmother.

"Indeed he will," replied the fairy, tapping the frog. And suddenly there was a coachman standing by the coach.

"All aboard!" he cried.

Cinderella was just about to leap inside when her godmother called her back. "I nearly forgot something," she said.

The tip of her wand touched Cinderella's ragged clothes and Cinderella looked down to see, to her astonishment, that she was wearing the most beautiful ballgown that there ever was. At her neck glittered a diamond necklace and on her feet were a dainty pair of glass slippers. "Have a lovely time at the ball," said her godmother. "But do not stay a minute longer than midnight, for on the stroke of twelve, everything will be as it was before."

And with that, she vanished.

When Cinderella arrived at the ball, she found herself in a dazzling ballroom filled with people. Everyone stopped to stare at this beautiful girl, and soon the prince himself approached and asked her to dance. "Who is she?" people were asking. The prince and Cinderella danced together all evening. Her stepsisters watched, never once guessing who she was.

"Isn't she beautiful," remarked the elder sister jealously.

"Such a tiny waist – she might snap in two!" whispered the other spitefully, and they both roared with laughter.

When the banquet was served the prince insisted that Cinderella sit next to him, and after dinner they danced again. Cinderella was enjoying herself so much she forgot all about the time. It was only when the clock struck midnight that she remembered her godmother's warning. She fled from the ballroom without a backward glance. The prince hurried after her but she ran faster than he. As she sped down the steps her ballgown turned to rags and she dropped one of her glass slippers. The prince picked it up. By the time she reached home, Cinderella was exhausted.

Soon her sisters arrived home. "There was the most beautiful princess at the ball," said one.

"The prince fell in love with her, and he was deeply saddened when she left at midnight," said the other.

As for the prince, he spent all night with the glass slipper pressed to his cheek, mourning the loss of the most wonderful girl he had ever set eyes upon. The next morning he was determined to find her. He sent his servant to all corners of the kingdom. "I will marry the girl whose foot fits the slipper," he declared. Well, every princess, duchess and lady in the land tried on the slipper, but none of them could fit the tiny shoe on her foot.

At last the servant called at the house of Cinderella and her stepsisters. "Me first!" they cried, pushing each other out of the way. One sister tried on the slipper but her toes were so fat that she couldn't squeeze them into the dainty shoe. Then the other sister tried, but her toes were so long they wouldn't fit either.

Cinderella had been watching from her corner by the fire. Now she came forward. "May I try on the shoe?" she asked timidly.

The stepsisters shrieked, "Don't be absurd! You weren't even at the ball."

But the prince's servant said, "If you wish to try on the slipper, then you shall." Cinderella slid her foot into the glass slipper and of course it fitted perfectly. The stepsisters were completely speechless with rage.

At that moment there was a flash of bright light and Cinderella's fairy godmother appeared. She touched Cinderella with her magic wand and immediately the girl's rags were transformed into the ballgown that she had worn the night before. Then her sisters recognised the beautiful princess they had seen at the ball. They fell upon their knees and begged forgiveness for the way they had treated her, hoping that they, too, might be invited to the palace. The servant escorted Cinderella to the palace and when the prince saw her, he immediately asked her to marry him. At the wedding there was much rejoicing and the sisters were so well behaved that they, too, received marriage proposals and they all lived happily ever after.

The Very Big Parcel

Once upon a time there lived an old man and his wife. They dwelled in a small house with a small, neat garden and they were very contented. What's more, they had very good friends and neighbours, with whom they shared everything. One day, there was a knock at the door and there stood the postman with a huge parcel in his arms.

"My, oh my!" exclaimed the old man to his wife as he staggered into the kitchen with the enormous load.

"Whatever can it be?" wondered the old woman as the two of them stared at the parcel. "Perhaps it's a new set of china," said she.

"Or a new wheelbarrow," said he. And they began to think about all the fancy things there might be inside the parcel.

"Well, why don't we open it and see?" said the old lady at last. And so they did. They looked into the box and at first it seemed to be totally empty.

"Well, I never did!" cried the old man. And then he spotted something right in the corner of the box. He lifted it out into the light to examine it more carefully and discovered it was a single seed.

Well, the old man and his wife were most upset. Whereas before they were quite content, now that they had thought about all the things that might have been in the box they were bitterly disappointed by the seed. "Still," said the old man at last, "we'd better plant it anyway. Who knows, maybe we'll get a nice fresh lettuce from it."

So he planted the seed in the garden. Every day he watered the ground and soon a shoot appeared. The shoot grew into a strong young plant and then it grew taller and taller. Higher and higher it grew until it was a handsome tree. The man and his wife were excited to see fruits growing on the tree. "I wonder if they're apples," the old man said. Each day he watered the tree and examined the fruits. One day he said to his wife, "The first fruit is ready to pick." He carefully reached up into the tree and picked the large red fruit.

He carried it into the kitchen and put it on the table. Then he took a knife and cut the fruit in half. To his astonishment out poured a pile of gold coins. "Come quickly!" he called to his wife. Well, the pair of them danced round the kitchen for joy.

The old couple decided to spend just one gold coin and keep the rest. "After all," said the woman wisely, "we don't know what's in the other fruits. They may be full of worms." So they spent one golden penny in the town and put the rest aside.

The next day the old man picked another big red fruit and this, too, was full of gold. After that the old couple were less careful with their money, thinking all the fruits must be full of gold.

They had a wonderful time buying fine clothes and things for the house and garden. Each day the man picked another fruit. Each day it was full of gold and each day they went into town and had a grand time spending the money. But all the while the man forgot entirely to water the tree.

Meanwhile, the old couple's friends and neighbours started to gossip among themselves. They wondered where all the money was coming from and they began to resent the old couple. They noticed that the old couple didn't buy anything for their friends, or even throw a party. Gradually their friends ignored them until the old couple were left with no friends at all. But they didn't even notice because they were so busy spending the gold coins.

Then one day the old man looked out into the garden and saw that the tree was all withered. He rushed outside and threw bucket after bucket of water over the tree, but all to no avail.

He and his wife frantically picked the fruits left on the tree, but when they took them indoors they found to their dismay that they were cracked and gnarled. When they broke open the fruits they were full of dust. "If only I had not been so thoughtless and remembered to water the tree!" cried the old man in anguish.

The next day the old couple looked out of the window to find that the tree had vanished. Now what were they to do? They had completely neglected to take care of their garden and now they had nothing to eat. They realised that they would have to sell their riches to buy food. Then they also needed new gardening tools, for theirs had grown rusty with neglect.

As the weeks passed, the old man and his wife gradually sold all the fine things they had bought, just to keep body and soul together. They felt truly miserable and sorry for the way they had treated their neighbours. For now they realised just how lonely they were without their friends. "We have no money now," said the wife one day, "but let's have a party anyway. For friendship is more valuable than any amount of gold coins."

So the old couple invited all their friends and neighbours round and they had a grand party. The friends wondered what had happened to all the old couple's riches and what had happened to make the old couple so friendly once more, but I don't think they ever found out, do you?

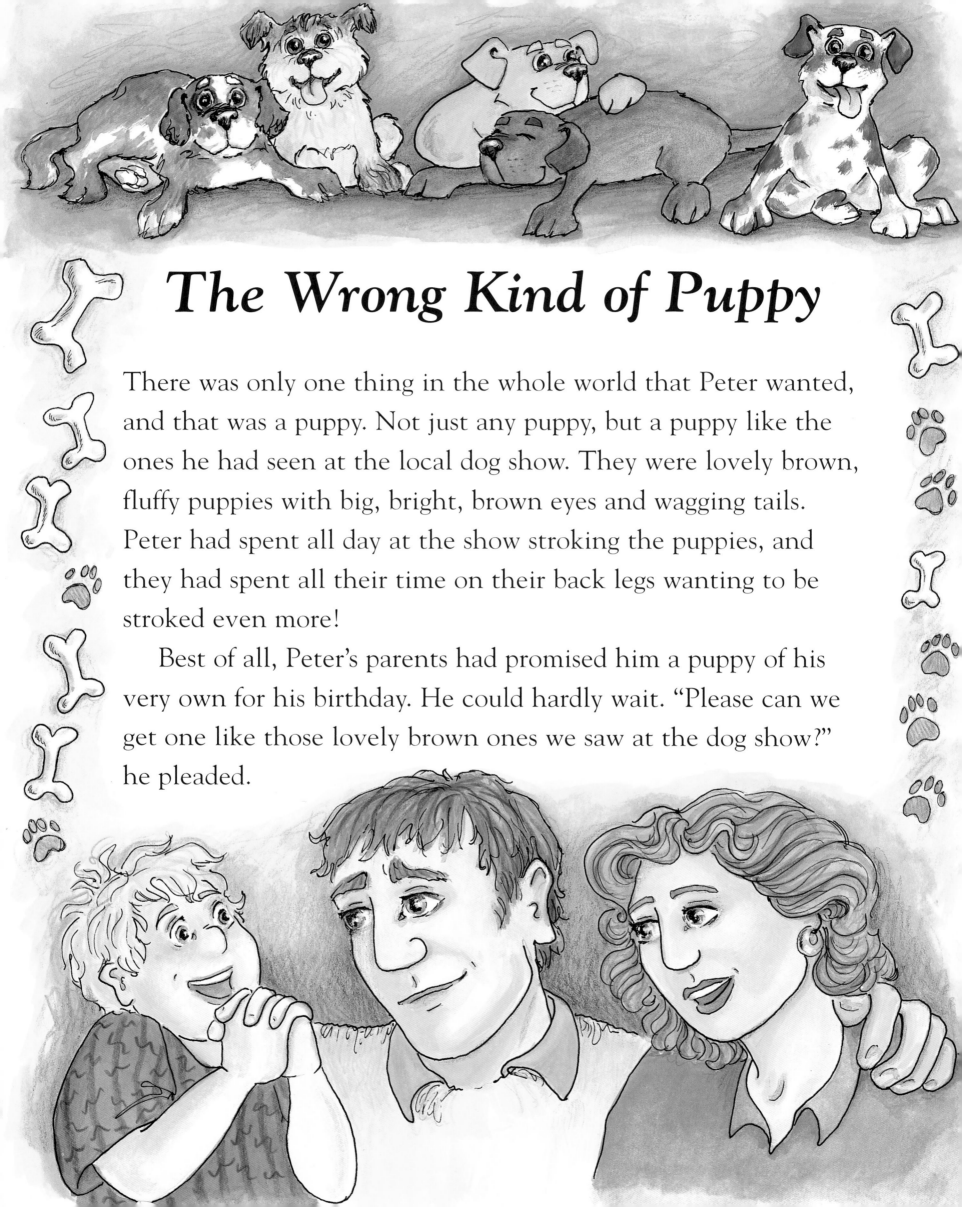

The Wrong Kind of Puppy

There was only one thing in the whole world that Peter wanted, and that was a puppy. Not just any puppy, but a puppy like the ones he had seen at the local dog show. They were lovely brown, fluffy puppies with big, bright, brown eyes and wagging tails. Peter had spent all day at the show stroking the puppies, and they had spent all their time on their back legs wanting to be stroked even more!

Best of all, Peter's parents had promised him a puppy of his very own for his birthday. He could hardly wait. "Please can we get one like those lovely brown ones we saw at the dog show?" he pleaded.

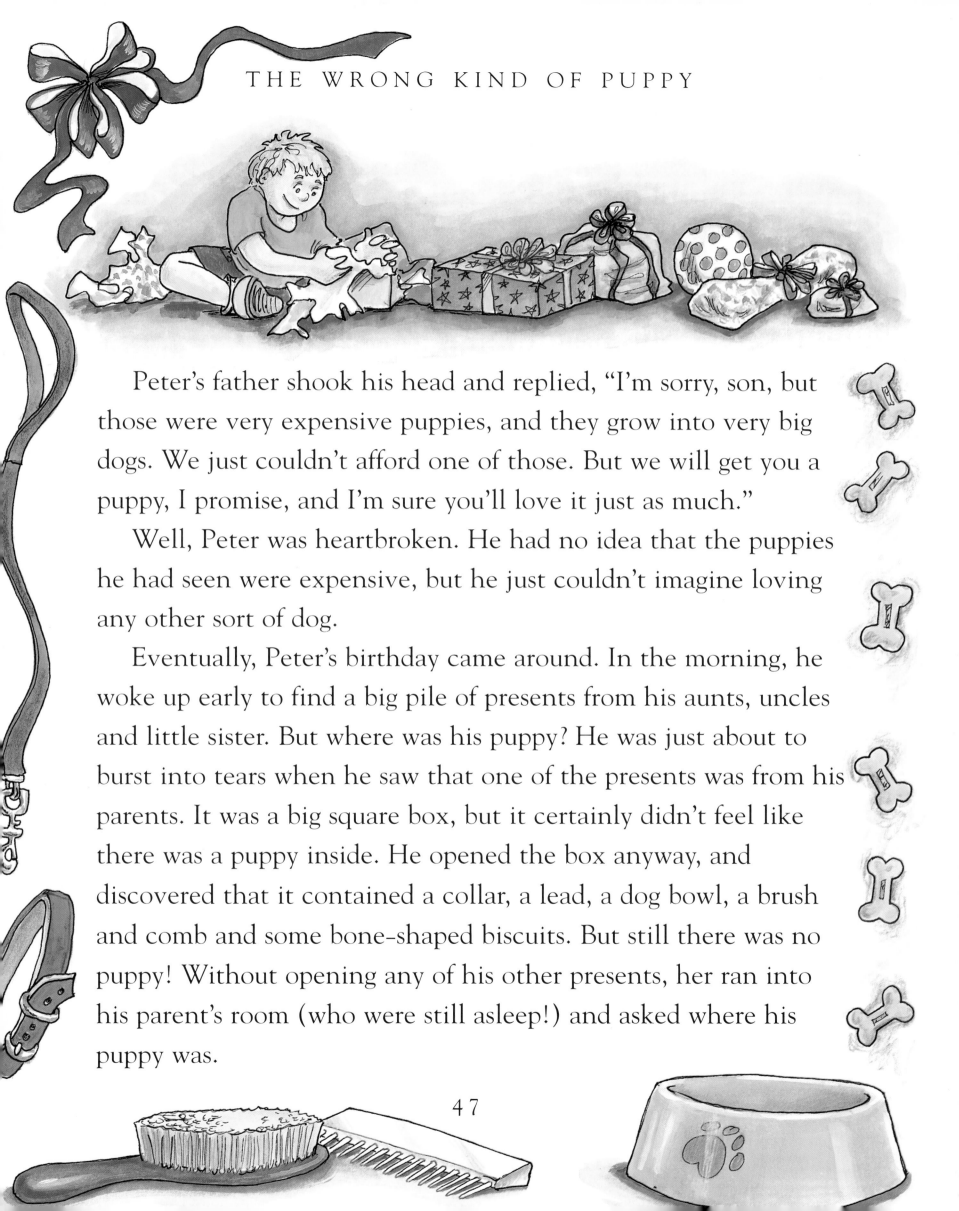

Peter's father shook his head and replied, "I'm sorry, son, but those were very expensive puppies, and they grow into very big dogs. We just couldn't afford one of those. But we will get you a puppy, I promise, and I'm sure you'll love it just as much."

Well, Peter was heartbroken. He had no idea that the puppies he had seen were expensive, but he just couldn't imagine loving any other sort of dog.

Eventually, Peter's birthday came around. In the morning, he woke up early to find a big pile of presents from his aunts, uncles and little sister. But where was his puppy? He was just about to burst into tears when he saw that one of the presents was from his parents. It was a big square box, but it certainly didn't feel like there was a puppy inside. He opened the box anyway, and discovered that it contained a collar, a lead, a dog bowl, a brush and comb and some bone-shaped biscuits. But still there was no puppy! Without opening any of his other presents, her ran into his parent's room (who were still asleep!) and asked where his puppy was.

47

"We have to go and collect it today," said his mother. "We've chosen you a lovely little puppy from the dogs' home that desperately needed a new family to look after it. We can go and get it as soon as we've had breakfast."

Peter was much too excited to eat any breakfast, of course, and spent the next half hour saying, "Can we go yet?" Eventually everyone was ready, and they all climbed into the car for the journey to the dogs' home. Peter sat in the back clutching the lead and hoping it wouldn't be too long before there was a puppy attached to the other end of it!

Soon they reached the dogs' home, and one of the kennel maids took them to where Peter's puppy was being kept. But when Peter first set eyes on the puppy, his heart sank. This wasn't anything like the sort of puppy he had wanted. Instead of being brown and fluffy and bouncy, this puppy was tiny and scraggy and timid. When it saw Peter and his family approach, it gave a little wag of its tail but then just stood in its cage whimpering.

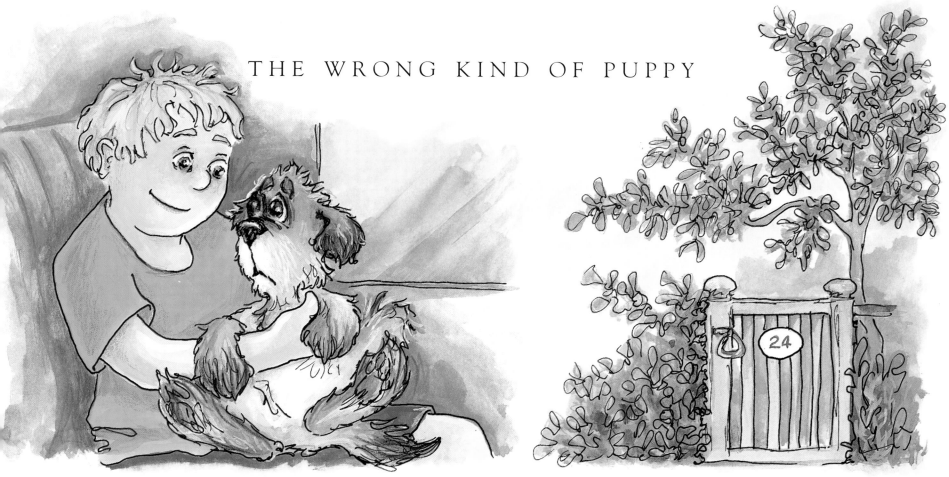

Now Peter had been taught by his parents that you must never be ungrateful for presents, even if they aren't exactly what you wanted. So although he was very disappointed, he reached out and stroked the puppy. The little scruffy puppy timidly approached Peter, licked his hand, and then ran off into the corner of the cage.

"He'll soon get used to you," said the kennel maid brightly. "Come on, Rags, time to go to your new home." And with that, she lifted the little puppy up and placed him in Peter's arms.

All the way home, the little puppy sat quietly in Peter's arms, occasionally trembling. Now and again he looked up at Peter with his big, soft eyes.

When they got Rags home, he was so frightened that he ran and hid under the curtains. Peter wondered how he was going to be able to play with such a timid friend.

Later that day Peter was sitting at the table having lunch when he felt something cold and wet against his leg; it was Rags's nose. He peered down to see Rags looking up at him, his tail wagging backwards and forwards. "He's looking a bit happier now," said Peter's father. "It will only be a matter of time before he feels really at home here."

The next morning, Peter hurried downstairs as soon as he awoke to say good morning to Rags – because the truth was, although Rags wasn't quite like the puppy he had expected, he was really getting very fond of him.

Rags jumped out of his basket when he saw Peter, his tail wagging furiously. "He's quite a waggy dog after all," thought Peter. Then Rags picked up his ball and began to play with it. Every time Peter tried to take it, Rags scurried off with a wag of his tail, looking round to make sure that Peter was chasing him. He seemed to like playing after all!

As the days went by, Rags seemed to grow more and more playful. He would jump up and greet his family with a big lick and a wagging tail, he always wanted to go for walks and to play, and he was very quick to learn tricks.

Peter just couldn't believe how much Rags had changed from the timid little creature in the dogs' home to the happy, playful puppy he was now – all thanks to a little love and care.

But the most curious thing of all was the puppy's appearance. He had now grown a beautiful, fluffy coat and, if Peter wasn't very much mistaken, it was quite brown, too. And it matched the colour of his big, brown eyes.

Rusty's Big Day

Long ago there lived a poor farmer called Fred, who had a horse called Rusty. Once Rusty had been a good, strong horse. He had willingly pulled the plough and taken his master into town to sell his vegetables. Now he was too old to work on the farm, but the farmer couldn't bear to think of getting rid of him because he was so sweet-natured. "It would be like turning away one of my own family," Fred used to say. Rusty spent his days grazing in the corner of the field. He was quite content, but he felt sad that he was no longer able to help the poor farmer earn his living.

One day, Fred decided to go to town to sell a few vegetables. He harnessed Beauty, the young mare, to the wagon and off they went. Beauty shook her fine mane and tossed a glance at Rusty as if to say, "Look who's queen of the farmyard!"

While Fred was in the town, his eye was caught by a notice pinned to a tree. It said:

> *Horse Parade at 2 pm today*
> *The winner will pull the king's carriage*
> *to the Grand Banquet tonight*

"There's not a moment to lose, my girl!" said Fred. "We must get you ready for the parade." So saying, he turned the wagon around. "Giddy-up, Beauty!" he called, and she trotted all the way back to the farm.

Fred set to work to make Beauty look more lovely than she had ever done before. He scrubbed her hoofs and brushed her coat until it shone. Then he plaited her mane and tied it with a bright red ribbon. Rusty watched from the field. "How fine she looks," he thought, wistfully. "She's sure to win." He felt a bit sad that he was too old to take part in the parade, so he found a patch of the sweetest grass to graze on, to console himself.

53

All at once, he heard Fred approach. "Come on, old boy," he said, "you can come, too. It'll be fun for you to watch the parade, won't it?" Rusty was thrilled. It seemed such a long time since the master had last taken him into town. Fred brushed Rusty's coat, too. "You want to look your best, don't you now, old boy?" he said.

Soon the three of them set off back into town, with Fred riding on Beauty's back and Rusty walking by their side. When they reached the parade ground, there were already a lot of horses gathered there with their owners. There were horses of every shape and size – small, skinny ones, big, muscular ones and there were even big, skinny ones, too!

Soon it was time for the parade to begin. The king entered the parade ground, followed by the members of the royal court. They took their places at one end of the ground. Then the king announced three contests. First there would be a race. The horses would gallop from one end of the parade ground to the other. Then there would be a contest of strength. Each horse would have to try and pull a heavy carriage. Lastly, there would be a trotting competition. Each horse would have to carry a rider around the parade ground.

The competition began. All the horses lined up at the starting line. "Come on, Rusty. Have a go!" whispered Fred. He led Rusty and Beauty to where the other horses were lined up.

All the other horses turned and stared. "What's an old horse like you doing taking part in a contest like this?" one of them asked disdainfully.

"You won't make it past the starting line!" taunted another.

Rusty said nothing and took his place at the start. Then they were off down the field. Rusty felt his heart pounding and his feet fly like never before, but try as he might he just couldn't keep up with the others and came in last.

"What did you expect?" snorted the other horses turning their backs on poor old Rusty.

However, Rusty was not downcast. "Speed isn't everything," he said to himself.

Now it was time for the test of strength. One by one the horses took it in turns to pull the carriage. When it was Rusty's turn, he tried his best. He felt every muscle in his aching body strain, as he slowly pulled the carriage along.

"Not a hope!" declared the other horses.

"Strength isn't everything," said Rusty to himself.

Next it was time for the trotting competition. "I shall ride each horse in turn," declared the king. He climbed up on to the first horse, but it bolted away so fast that the king was left hanging by the stirrups. The next horse lifted his legs so high that he threw the king right up in the air and he might have hurt himself badly, if he hadn't been caught by one of his courtiers. The next horse was so nervous about carrying the king that his teeth chattered, and the king had to put his fingers in his ears. Then it was Beauty's turn and she carried the king magnificently, until she stumbled at the end. At last it was Rusty's turn. The other horses sniggered, "Let's see that old horse make a fool of himself!"

RUSTY'S BIG DAY

Rusty carried the king quite slowly and steadily, making sure he picked his feet up carefully, so that his royal highness would not be jolted. "Thank you for a most pleasant ride," said the king dismounting. There was a hush as the horses and their owners awaited the result of the contest. "I have decided," announced the king, "that Rusty is the winner. Not only did he give me a most comfortable ride, but he accepted his other defeats with dignity. Speed and strength are not everything, you know."

Rusty and Fred were overjoyed, and even Beauty offered her congratulations. "Though I might have won if I hadn't stumbled," she muttered.

So Rusty proudly pulled the king's carriage that evening, and he made such a good job of it that the king asked him if he would do it again the following year. Then the king asked Fred if his daughter could ride Beauty from time to time. He even gave Fred a bag of gold to pay for the horses' upkeep. So the three of them were happy as they never had been before as they returned home to the farm that night.

The King Who Ate Too Much

Long ago, in a kingdom far, far away, there lived a greedy king. Now the thing that this king loved, more than anything else in the whole world, was food. He simply couldn't get enough of it. Ever since he was a little prince, he had been allowed to eat whatever he wanted, whenever he wanted it. And because he was always eating, he just got fatter and fatter and fatter with every day that passed.

When he became king, his appetite seemed to get even bigger! As soon as he woke in the morning, he would have his servants bring him an enormous breakfast. After eating several huge, steaming bowls of porridge, he would eat slice after slice of hot, buttered toast and jam, followed by all the boiled eggs that the royal chickens could lay.

In case he got a little hungry mid-morning, he would have a snack – usually ten or more chocolate cakes, washed down with as many cups of tea!

At lunchtime, the table would groan with the weight of all the pies, sandwiches, fruit and biscuits that the greedy king was about to gobble down.

For afternoon tea, it would be cakes, cakes and more cakes.

But the king's biggest meal was supper! The royal cooks toiled for most of the day to prepare this feast. When it was time for the king to eat, one servant after another would carry in great bowls of steaming soup, plates of fish of every kind, followed by huge roasts and dishes of vegetables. Down it all went, followed by fruit and jelly. At last, the king would be full and he would retire to his bed for the night.

But the king's greedy eating habits also made him a very thoughtless king. No-one dared tell him that much of the wealth of the kingdom had to be spent on his huge meals. In the meantime, his loyal subjects were going hungry and becoming poor and needy.

One day, just after the king had eaten his usual big lunch, he began to feel very strange. Not only did he feel even bigger than usual, he also began to feel very light. Suddenly, without any warning, he started floating up from the table and into the air like a big balloon.

"Help! Get me down!" he cried.

The royal courtiers and servants jumped up and down and tried in vain to grab the king as he floated upwards, but in no time at all he had floated out of reach. Before anyone knew it, he had floated out of the castle window. Out across the royal grounds he went, over the river and towards the woods and mountains of his kingdom.

"Wooaa-aaah!" cried the king, as he disappeared from view.

Soon, the king began to float over a small farm. He looked down and saw the farmer's children, dressed only in rags, searching for firewood. Some thin, hungry cows stood nearby chewing on a few meagre pieces of hay.

Over the next farm he floated, and a similar sad scene met his gaze. Dressed in rags, a poor farmer and his family toiled their soil hoping to grow enough to eat.

Next he floated over a small village. Everywhere he looked he saw shabby, run-down houses in need of repair and people in the streets begging for money.

Every farm and every village the king floated over told the same story of hunger and misery. The king suddenly felt very sad and very ashamed. He had been so busy enjoying himself eating that he hadn't given a thought to the plight of his subjects. While he was getting fatter and fatter, they were all getting thinner and poorer.

Now, a gust of wind was blowing the king back towards his castle. As he was passing over the castle, he suddenly felt himself falling. Down, down, he went until he landed back into the castle grounds with a great thud and a bounce.

That very day, the king sent out a royal proclamation. All his loyal subjects were to come to the castle for a huge feast, after which they would all be given a purse full of gold.

As for the king, he was never greedy again. Instead of spending all his money on food for himself, he gave enough to all the people in the land so that they would never be hungry or poor again.